THE BAT
ALL IN A FLAP!

DON CONROY

Artist, storyteller, wildlife expert and TV
presenter, Don's talents are very varied.
His book *Cartoon Fun*, in which he shows
how to draw cartoons, was a runaway
bestseller. He has also written and illustrated
a popular trilogy based on wildlife:
On Silent Wings, *Wild Wings* and *Sky Wings*.

OTHER BOOKS IN THIS SERIES

The Owl Who Couldn't Give a Hoot!
The Tiger Who Was a Roaring Success!
The Hedgehog's Prickly Problem!

For Justine

THE BAT WHO WAS ALL IN A FLAP!

Written and illustrated by

DON CONROY

THE O'BRIEN PRESS
DUBLIN

This revised edition first published 1995
by The O'Brien Press Ltd.,
20 Victoria Road, Rathgar, Dublin 6, Ireland.
First edition published 1992.
This edition produced specially for School Book Fairs Ltd., 1996.
Copyright text and illustrations © Don Conroy

BRITISH LIBRARY CATALOGUING-IN-PUBLICATION DATA
Conroy, Don
The Bat Who Was All In A Flap!
I. Title
823.914 [J]

The O'Brien Press receives assistance from
The Arts Council / An Chomhairle Ealaíon.

ISBN 0-86278-416-6

2 4 6 8 10 9 7 5 3
96 98 00 02 04 03 01 99 97

Cover illustration: Don Conroy
Cover design: O'Brien Press
Cover separations: Lithoset, Dublin
Printed and bound in Great Britain by
Cox & Wyman Ltd, Reading, Berkshire

One sunny
morning in
autumn, Harry
Hedgehog yawned
and stretched.

Time to get up, he thought, rubbing
the sleep from his eyes. He hopped
out of bed and moved to the middle of
the floor. Now for some hedgehog
exercises, he thought.

He touched his toes three times from
a standing position. 'That should be
enough.'

Then he lay down on his front and began to do some press-ups, but he only managed four before collapsing in a heap! 'No need to strain myself!' Old Lepus, the wise old hare, had told him that exercise was good, especially in the morning. Harry splashed cold water all over himself. 'Brrr! that's cold.' Then he shook himself like a dog, standing on one leg and shaking the other, then swapping positions. 'Completely dry,' he announced.

He looked at himself in the mirror, checking his spines. There were leaves and bits of grass stuck to his back. 'Wow! What a messy back!' he thought.

Taking a brush he began to move it up and down his back. 'Aaah! That feels good.' Then he noticed a pile of spines on the floor.

'Oh no! I must have rubbed myself too hard. I'll be bald!'

He ran to the mirror again and checked his back carefully. Then he gave a sigh of relief.

'You'd never notice. Well, when you have over five thousand spines, losing a few here and there should make no difference.'

Not that he'd ever counted his spines. It was Old Lepus who'd told him how many spines he had, and *he* knew everything – well, almost everything.

Harry put on his waistcoat. This was a gift from the old hare and it certainly helped keep his back fairly clear of grasses and leaves, and kept him warm on these chilly autumn mornings.

Harry was ready to face the day.

'Boy, I'm hungry,' he said. 'What can I find for breakfast?' He searched the cupboard. 'Empty! Oh no!' Then, looking out the window at the leaves dancing in the wind, he thought: 'Ah yes! That's it! I'll visit the old orchard. There's sure to be lots to eat there!' His mouth watered just thinking about all those juicy apples and pears.

He set off. The day was very blustery, and a sycamore leaf flew straight into his face and another onto his head.

'Do you mind!' he said to the wind. 'I've just brushed my spines!' Another one stuck to his bottom.

'Oh bother! At least there will be shelter in the orchard.'

'Hello, Harry,' called a voice from behind him. Harry looked around to see his good friend Renny Fox padding up the woodland path. 'Windy, isn't it!' said Renny.

'Oh yes,' said Harry, feeling the chill. 'It's what my uncle calls a *lazy* wind.'

The fox looked blankly at Harry. 'Lazy?'

'You see,' explained Harry, 'it would rather go through you than go around you!'

Renny laughed loudly. 'That's a good one! I must tell it to my cousins. I'm off to visit them tomorrow. They live near the mountains. It's my uncle Redcote's birthday and there's a party. You know, they live near a wishing well.'

'Really!' said Harry. 'Does it work?'

'Well, my uncle believes it does. He told me about the time his brother had his brush shot off completely by an angry farmer. He made a wish by the well and the very next day he grew a fine new bushy tail!'

'Amazing!' said Harry. 'I remember once making a wish when I saw a shooting star.'

'And did it come true?' asked Renny.

'I don't know,' said Harry.

'What do you mean, you don't know?'

'Well, I couldn't remember what I'd wished for!'

Renny laughed, and looked up at the swallows gathering on the wires preparing for their long flight to Africa. 'Did you ever wish you could fly? It would be nice, wouldn't it?'

'Why don't you make a wish at the wishing well for the power of flight?' said Harry.

'I might just do that.'

Another leaf landed on Harry's head. 'Oh, I just remembered. I'm on my way to the old orchard. Do you want to come?'

'Great idea!' said Renny.

'Let's go!'

They sneaked in through an opening in the old stone wall.

'Look at all those trees laden with that juicy fruit,' said Renny, licking his lips.

'I see half the thrush families have had the same idea. Look at them all – the mistle and the song thrushes – and then the blackbirds, robins, and those visitors the redwings and fieldfares too. Still, there should be enough for everyone!' said Harry.

'I thought I might find you here,' said Sammy Squirrel, hopping over. He was busy collecting nuts.

Renny decided to feed on the blackberries that grew along the wall.

Harry checked out the apples and tried to carry away as many as possible. He could only manage two at a go, because every time he picked up an extra apple one of the others would fall.

'Why don't you take off your waistcoat and use it as a carrier?' suggested Billy Blackbird, who was watching from a nearby pear tree.

'Good idea!' said Harry. 'Thanks, Billy.'

Laying the waistcoat on the grass, Harry placed five apples on it and pulled them over to the wall. There he began to make a big pile.

Then when he went back to the trees a pear landed on his head! 'Ouch!' he yelled, then 'Ouch!' again as another struck him. The two pears stuck onto his spines.

'That's what's called using your head,' said Sammy.

The
hedgehog
continued to stick
more apples and
pears onto his coat. Then he
lay back to admire his work, and
another couple of apples that were
lying on the ground by the tree trunk
stuck to his back. When he tried to
move he found he couldn't.

'Help!' he yelled. 'Help! I'm stuck!'

Sammy climbed down the tree trunk
and pulled Harry up onto his feet.
Harry staggered over to the wall with
the apples and pears stuck to him. He
gave a good shake and the fruit fell off.

'Clever, don't you think?' he remarked, very pleased with himself.

They collected fruit all morning. In the afternoon Bentley Badger came and helped too. After they had made several mounds of fruit Renny suggested they should take some to Old Lepus who could make delicious apple and pear tarts.

Ollie Otter came into the orchard
with a bag he had found near the river.
'Hi, gang!' he said. 'I just thought I'd
collect some apples for Old Lepus.'

'Great minds think alike!' said
Bentley, and he began to fill the bag. It
took Renny and Bentley all their
strength to drag the bagful of fruit to
Lepus's home.

The old hare was delighted to see his friends again, and doubly delighted to receive the bag of goodies. 'I think I'll make some apple and pear tarts,' he declared.

'That's just what we hoped you'd say,' said Sammy.

'Well, no sooner said than done.'

'And there are more where they came from,' said Harry proudly. 'I made a big pile of apples and pears just beside the wall of the orchard.'

It was dark when the tarts were ready and the sweet smells wafted through the woods.

'Tarts ready!' called the old hare. 'Come and get them!'

They all sat around and began to feast on the delicious pies. The next minute Otus and Barny swooped in.

'Greetings, everyone!' called the two owls.

'I thought birds had a poor sense of smell,' said Harry, biting into a large slice of tart.

'Yes, that's true,' said Barny, 'but we have excellent eyesight and we saw you all stuffing yourselves from the woods.'

'Come and join us,' said Old Lepus. 'There's plenty.'

After they had all eaten their fill they headed for home, thanking Old Lepus for the wonderful supper.

'I must thank all of *you*, for without the fruit there would be no delicious pies.'

Renny was given one to take to his uncle.

On the way home, Ollie Otter suddenly slipped and landed in the bracken.

Harry laughed loudly. 'Sorry, Ollie, I shouldn't laugh, but you do look so funny.' Then he too slipped, shot up in the air and landed beside Ollie.

'What's the matter with you two?'
asked Bentley – and then *he* went into
a slide and fell on top of the others.

'Ouch! Aaah! You nearly flattened
me!' yelled Harry.

Sammy Squirrel arrived on the scene and giggled to see his friends piled on top of each other. Then he swung down from the tree, slipped and fell on top of them all!

'The ground must be very icy. *That* must be the reason,' said Bentley.

'Icy!' exclaimed Harry. 'Don't be silly. It's not *that* cold. It's

the dew! It makes the grass very
slippery!'

'Excuse me, friends,' said Otus the
long-eared owl, who was sitting on a
branch beside Barny. 'But your trouble
is not ice or dew. It's this!' He held up
a banana skin.

'A banana skin!' said the others. 'How
did that get here?'

'Hey look!' said Harry. 'There are
banana skins everywhere.'

'Who could have dropped them?' asked Ollie.

'Very strange indeed,' said Bentley.

'Maybe there's a banana tree in the orchard,' suggested Sammy.

'No,' said Harry. 'I've never seen bananas growing around here. The weather would not be that *appealing*.'

'Oh, that's good all right,' laughed Ollie. 'A-peeling!'

'Yes,' said Harry proudly, 'I thought you might like it. I do come out with some good jokes, even if I say so myself.'

'None of this explains why the skins are scattered about,' said Bentley seriously.

'I think we should go home and
sleep on it,' suggested Ollie.

'Mind where you walk,' warned
Harry. 'There could be more ... oops!'
As he turned to go he stepped into a
rabbit hole.

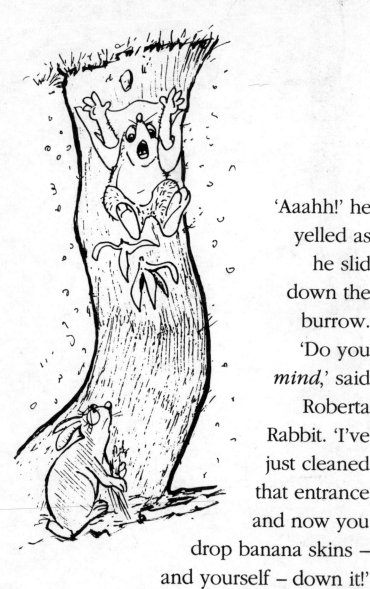

'Aaahh!' he yelled as he slid down the burrow. 'Do you *mind*,' said Roberta Rabbit. 'I've just cleaned that entrance and now you drop banana skins – and yourself – down it!'

'Sorry, Roberta, but I don't eat
bananas. I mean, I didn't drop them.
Well, I did drop in myself, but that was
an accident –'

'Oh never mind,' said Roberta. 'But
would you be so kind as to leave? The
bunnies are sleeping.'

Harry quickly scrambled up out of the
burrow. 'I don't know about anyone
else, but I'm ready for bed. Goodnight,
everyone!' And he shuffled off.

When Harry arrived home he was very tired. But climbing into bed he began to wonder again about those banana skins. 'They must have been dropped by some untidy human,' he decided.

There was a bright moon in the sky. What a lovely ring around the moon, he thought. He yawned, then noticed something fly past the moon. 'I see Renny's out flying in the moonlight,' he said. 'Very nice ...' He turned over to go to sleep.

Suddenly he sat up, rubbed his eyes, and stared out the window.

'*Renny flying!* Am I dreaming? No, I'm not. Sure I didn't even get to sleep yet. Could I be ha... oh dear! What's that word? Ha... ha... No, that's a laugh! *Hallucinating!* That's it. I'm ha... I'm not going to say it again, but I must be doing it, for whoever heard of a flying fox? I'll just go to sleep now and tomorrow I'll laugh at the very idea of Renny flying!'

But there was a sudden tap at the door. Harry hid under the covers. Then came another tap, louder this time. Tap! Tap!

'I'm asleep,' yelled Harry. 'Oh dear! I shouldn't have said that! Whoever knocked will know I'm awake now.'

Then a face appeared at the window.

'Aaah!' shrieked the hedgehog, and he jumped under his bed.

'Hello, Harry! It's me, Barny. Hope I didn't wake you.'

Harry opened the door. 'Barny! You nearly scared the wits out of me.'

'Sorry!' said the barn owl. 'But you'll never believe what I just saw!'

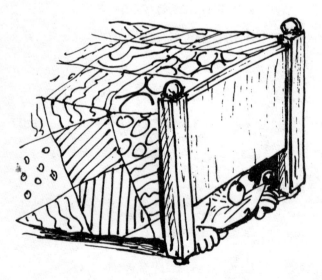

'Don't tell me,' said Harry. 'A fox
flying!'

'Yes, that's right!' said Barny.

'I knew it! I knew it!' exclaimed
Harry. 'I was not ha... ha...'

'You were not laughing?' asked Barny.

'No! I was not ha... *dreaming*. We both saw it! So it *must* be true. We must tell the others that Renny has the power of flight!'

'Renny?' asked Barny.

'Yes. He went to visit his relations and they have a wishing well. He must have wished for the power of flight – and got it!'

'Well, you could blow me down with a feather,' said Barny. 'Renny can fly!'

'We'll meet tomorrow at Three Rock and tell everyone about it. Pass the word around.'

'Right,' said Barny, then he flew out into the silent night.

Early in the morning Harry went to the orchard to check on his pile of apples and pears. But when he arrived he found that the pile was reduced to a scattering of apple and pear cores. 'I wonder who ate my pile of fruit?' he said, annoyed.

'G'day, mate!' said a voice from behind him.

The hedgehog looked around and to his amazement he saw the fox hanging upside down on a branch.

'Renny, what are you doing hanging upside down like a bat?'

'I *am* a bat, mate.'

'You're gone batty, all right!' said Harry. 'I don't think it was such a good idea asking for that wish.'

'Wish? I wish I was back home. I miss my mates and my roost.'

41

'You're talking very strangely,' said Harry. 'It must be because you're hanging upside down.'

'Listen, mate, there's only one person around here talking funny, and it isn't me! I don't know how a fella is to get some sleep with all this chatter.' Then, as quick as a flash he flew over the wall towards the woods.

Sammy came along the wall to join Harry.

'You look very worried,' said Sammy. 'What's the matter?'

'I'm worried about Renny,' said Harry. 'He's acting very peculiar.'

Sammy and Harry went to Three Rock. There they met Bentley, Ollie, Billy, Barny and Otus.

'What's the urgent meeting about?' asked Bentley.

'Well, it's to do with Renny,' explained Harry. 'He's been acting very odd – flying and hanging upside down down from trees.'

'Don't be silly,' said Bentley. 'Renny can't fly.'

'I wish I could,' said a voice from the undergrowth.

They all looked around, and Renny Fox came padding over to them.

'Tell them!' demanded Harry. 'Tell them how you flew over the trees and spent the morning sleeping upside down and how you ate all the pears and apples I collected.'

Renny looked blankly at him. 'Me?' he said.

'And then you put on a funny voice to try and fool me!' said Harry. 'Admit it! You went to the wishing well and wished for the power of flight. And you got it.'

Renny turned around. 'My dear
friend, can you see any wings on me?'
he asked.

The others laughed.

Then Barny said nervously: '*I* saw
you flying too.'

'I have no recollection of ever flying,'
said the fox.

'Maybe it happens when you're asleep and you don't realise it?' suggested Sammy.

'Do you think so?' asked Renny, who by now was getting worried.

'Well, I suppose it's possible,' said Bentley. 'Especially if you were playing around with magic.'

'All I did was drink the water,' said Renny. 'I didn't make any wishes, honest.'

'But you did with me,' said Harry. 'Don't you remember saying when you saw the swallows that you wished you could fly? Maybe the wish was still in your head when you drank the water.'

'Oh dear,' sighed Renny. 'This can't
be right – if I sprout wings when I go
to sleep and raid the orchard and take
other people's apples and then sleep
upside down like a bat – oh no, it's all
too much.'

'Do you feel dizzy?' asked Harry.

'Why should I?' asked Renny.

'Well, with all the hanging upside
down it's sure to make you feel
strange.'

Renny felt his head. 'I think I *am*
feeling dizzy – and a little strange.'

'There's one way we can sort this out,' said Otus, the long-eared owl. 'Let's get Renny to sleep and we'll stay awake and see if he's sleep-flying. I've done it several times myself – sleep-flying. I crashed into a tree once – a very sore thing, indeed,'

'Are you feeling tired, Renny?' asked Ollie.

'No, but I'll try to sleep,' said Renny.

The fox lay on the ground, and the others sat around watching him. Renny yawned and stretched, then settled into his favourite position for sleep. They all watched carefully.

'Is he asleep?' whispered Harry.

'Give him a chance,' said Bentley.

They sat waiting. Then Harry began to whistle.

'Quiet!' said Sammy.

Renny sat up. 'It's no use. I'm not a bit tired.'

Ollie suggested that someone should sing a lullaby. Billy Blackbird offered, then cleared his throat and sang a beautiful song of twilight.

Soon Sammy began to feel sleepy and nodded off. Harry was snoring in a matter of seconds. Then the rest of the woodland friends lay down and slept soundly, even the owls.

All except Renny. He was too anxious to relax, let alone sleep.

'Nice try, Billy,' said the fox. 'But I just cannot get to sleep.' As he was talking he noticed that Billy had put himself to sleep too with his own lullaby!

'That's great! They're all asleep except me!'

'Good evening, mate!' said a voice from above.

Renny looked up and to his amazement there was a flying fox! It landed beside him.

'Good evening, mate! Nice evening. Don't suppose you have a few bananas on you? Or figs? I just love bananas and figs. They're my favourites.'

'A *flying fox*!' said Renny.

'How very observant of you, mate. I certainly am a flying fox, and proud of it. You're one of those red foxes?'

There was no reply. Renny had passed out with shock.

The others woke up and they couldn't believe their eyes either.

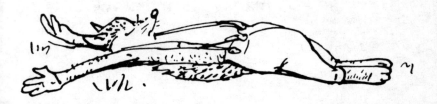

'Hey, you guys! No need to alarm yourselves. I'm only looking for a banana or two ...'

'See!' said Harry. 'A flying fox! I told you so. How do you do it, Renny?'

'Listen, mate, the name is *Lenny*, not Renny. Don't suppose any of you guys would have a banana?'

'Look,' said Sammy, 'there's Renny lying over there!'

'Wake up, Renny!' said Ollie.

'What's going on?' Renny asked nervously, rubbing his eyes.

'That's a clever trick,' said Harry. 'How did you manage to make two of you?'

'Listen! I've never seen that guy
before,' insisted Renny.

'Look, mates, I'm all in a flap. All I
know is that at the last full moon I was
feeding on a banana tree. I must have
eaten too much and fallen asleep.

When I woke up I was stuck in a box with lots of bunches of bananas, on a banana boat, and from there I was put into a truck. I didn't get out until some woman opened the box. I can still hear her screams as I flapped over her head and flew out the window. I didn't stop till I arrived here.'

'Can all foxes fly where you come from?' asked Ollie.

'Most of them.'

'If you don't mind my saying so,' said Bentley, 'you look more like a bat to me than a fox. No offence ...' he added quickly.

'There is only one way to find out who or what you are, and that's to ask the bats who live around here,' suggested Ollie.

They all agreed and stopped several bats in the neighbourhood.

The pipistrelle bat, which was the smallest in the area, said the flying fox was no relation of theirs.

The long-eared bat was next on the list and it just flapped away in fright when it saw Lenny!

The lesser horseshoe bat was not much help either, saying if the stranger was a bat he should be eating insects, not fruit. Then it flew away after a moth.

'Oh dear me. I'm afraid I don't belong. I'm not accepted as a fox and I'm not accepted as a bat. I'm nothing more than a freak around here.' Lenny flapped away slowly and rested on top of a Douglas fir tree.

'Poor fellow!' said Renny. 'What can we do to help him? Let's go to Old Lepus. He's the wise one around here.'

'Hey! Lenny!' yelled Harry. 'Can you come down here for a minute? We'd like you to meet someone.'

'No thanks, mate. I know when I'm
not wanted. No need to be polite.'

'What are we going to do?' asked
Bentley. 'We must convince him to
come with us to Old Lepus.'

'I have an idea,' said Barny, and quickly flew up to Lenny. The two of them flew back immediately. 'We're ready. Let's go!' said Barny.

'That was quick,' said Sammy, as they hurried to the old hare's home.

Old Lepus was just taking some blackberry pies out of the oven when they called. 'Good evening, everyone,' he said. 'You must have smelled the pies.'

'Mmmmm ... great!' said Sammy.

'Come in and have some supper. There's enough for everyone.' Old Lepus hadn't even noticed Lenny, and he began to slice up one of the tarts.

'Lepus,' said Renny. 'Can you help us? We have a slight problem –'

'I'm not that slight,' whispered Lenny.

'Well, a problem shared is a problem halved,' said Old Lepus.

'No-one is going to cut me in half!' yelled Lenny, watching Old Lepus holding the knife.

Old Lepus got quite a start when Lenny flapped his wings. 'Amazing!' said the hare. 'How very curious!'

'Listen, mate,' said Lenny, 'I'm no curiosity anywhere except here. Back home I'm just as ordinary as the rest. Who could have thought that eating a few bananas could get one into so much trouble? By the way, you don't by any chance have a few bananas lying about?'

'Of course,' said Old Lepus, handing him a bunch.

'So it was you who threw all those banana skins all over the place,' said Bentley.

'I never said I was a tidy eater!' retorted Lenny. 'I don't know, guys – I guess I'm good for nothing. Everything I do seems to cause problems, and all I'm doing is being myself.'

'Well,' said Old Lepus, 'all I can say
is that you are by far the most
interesting visitor we've had in these
parts since the Bengal tiger.'
'Blimey! You had a tiger
here!' said Lenny.

'Can you solve the mystery, Lepus?' asked Ollie. 'Is he a fox or a bat?'

'Oh, that's easy,' said Old Lepus, cutting another tart and passing slices around. 'He's called a flying fox, but he really is a fruit bat.'

'So we were *all* right,' said Ollie.

'And I wasn't ha... ha... hal... er imagining it after all. That's good anyway,' said Harry, pleased with himself.

'Well, all I know is whether I'm called a flying fox or a fruit bat it all boils down to the same thing.'

'What's that?' asked Sammy.

'That I'm good for nothing! I can't live with the other bats here because I'm too big. Besides, they eat insects, which is not my idea of supper. And I cannot live in a den like you, Renny. It would just cramp my style.'

'Well, maybe you should return home,' said Otus. 'All your family and friends are there.'

'That's a darned good idea,' agreed Lenny. 'I'll fly home in the morning.'

'So now this little mystery is over and we can all eat,' said Old Lepus.

'Don't mind if I do,' said Lenny. 'Cheers, mate!' Then he polished off a large slice of tart.

When they had finished eating, Lenny told them wonderful stories about his homeland, which is called Australia – about the kangaroos who carry their young in a pouch below their tummy and how they hop everywhere, about the koalas that climb trees, the kookaburra bird which has a silly laugh, the strange snakes and lizards and the beautiful bee-eater birds which have the colours of the rainbow on their feathers.

The woodland friends had a wonderful evening listening to the many tales Lenny had to relate about his homeland.

'When I get home maybe I should change my diet and leave those bananas alone,' announced Lenny.

'Perhaps I should acquire a taste for moths and insects! Yuck!' He shuddered at the very idea.

'There's no need to do that,' said Old Lepus. 'Because you eat bananas and all the other different fruits, you and your friends help to spread forests of fruit trees by dropping the seeds everywhere.'

'We *do*?' said Lenny blankly.

'You certainly do,' said the old hare.
'So keep on eating those bananas.'

'But not around here!' said Harry
with a smile.

'I'm a clever fella after all,' said Lenny
proudly. 'Thank you, mates, for
making me feel so useful, and for your
kindness.'

By first light the fruit bat was off.
They all watched him sail over the
treetops.

'G'day, mates!' he yelled as he
flapped away.

Harry asked Barny how he had managed to persuade the bat to come with them to Old Lepus's home.

'Oh, that was easy,' said Barny. 'I just told him there were lots of bananas there!'

'Well, I guess that's the last we'll see of the bat who was all in a flap!' said Renny, chuckling.